NOTE TO PARENTS

Learning to read is an important skill for all children. It is a big milestone that you can help your child reach. The Richard Scarry Easy Reader program is designed to support you and your child through this process. Developed by reading specialists, each book in the series includes carefully selected words and sentence structures to help children advance from beginner to intermediate to proficient readers.

Here are some tips to keep in mind as you read these books with your child:

First, preview the book together. Read the title. Then look at the cover. Ask your child, "What is happening on the cover? What do you think this book is about?"

Next, skim through the pages of the book and look at the illustrations. This will help your child use the illustrations to understand the story.

Then encourage your child to read. If he or she stumbles over words, try some of these strategies:

- **Use the pictures as clues**
- **Point out words that are repeated**
- **Sound out difficult words**
- **Break up bigger words into smaller chunks**
- **Use the context to lend meaning**

Finally, find out if your child understands what he or she is reading. After you have finished reading, ask, "What happened in this book?"

Above all, understand that each child learns to read at a different rate. Make sure to praise your young reader and provide encouragement along the way!

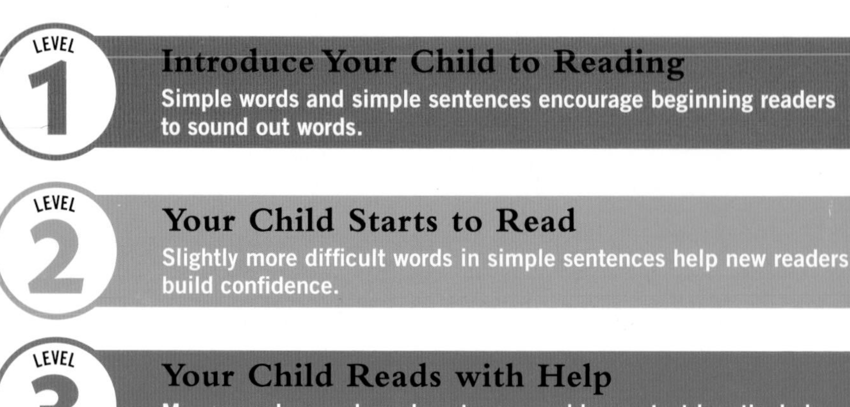

Kooky Campout

Illustrated by Huck Scarry
Written by Erica Farber

STERLING CHILDREN'S BOOKS
New York

It was the first day of summer. Hooray! Lowly wanted to play marbles.

Skip wanted to play ball.

Arthur wanted to play cards.

"Let's go camping!" said Huckle.

Huckle got a tent.

Skip got sleeping bags.

Lowly got fishing poles.

Arthur got snacks.

The boys set up the tent in the backyard.

In went the sleeping bags.

In went the snacks. In went the boys.

Don’t eat all the chips, Arthur!

CRASH! The tent fell.
The girls looked over the fence.
“What are you doing?”
asked Bridget.
“Camping,” said Huckle. “We are
going to sleep in our tent.”
“We want to go
camping, too,”
said Ella.

“We want to sleep in our tent,
too,” said Molly and Frances.

The girls set up their tent next door.
They put lots of things inside.
Ella and Molly had a tea party.
Arthur came, too.
"Would you like a cookie?" Ella
asked her doll.
"Yes," said Arthur. "I love cookies."

Then they had a pillow fight.
OOPS! Look out for the teacups!

The boys went fishing.
“I’m going to catch that fish,”
said Skip.
“I’m going to catch it,” said Huckle.
“That is not a fish,” said Molly.
“That is a shoe.”
“I got it!” said Arthur.
“I got it!”
said Lowly.

SPLASH! The boys fell into the pool! The shoe flew up in the air.

"We got it!" yelled the girls.

After dinner, it was time to catch fireflies.
Oh, no! Look where you are going, Huckle!

Mrs. Cat made them a campfire.
They roasted marshmallows.
Something strange ran by.

“It’s a monster!” yelled Ella.
She bumped into Arthur. Oh, no!
Marshmallows went everywhere!

“That is not a monster,” said
Bridget. “That is Arthur’s lizard.”
Then Lowly told a ghost joke.
Everyone laughed.

Molly told a ghost story.

"Once there was a ghost called Kooky. Kooky was very spooky. Kooky the Spooky Ghost came out at night. Do you know what Kooky said?"

"What?" asked Frances.

"I want a kooky! *Kooky* is how Kooky the Spooky Ghost said cookie."

CRASH! Everyone looked up.
They saw a spooky shadow.
CRUNCH! CRUNCH!
The spooky shadow was
eating something.
"It's Kooky the Spooky Ghost!"
said Molly.

AAAHHH! Everyone ran outside.

They saw cookies on the ground.

"It's Kooky the Spooky Ghost!"

they all yelled.

"Look!" said Huckle.

He pointed to the tent.

A small shape was standing in front of it. The small shape was eating a cookie. When it moved, the big shadow on the tent moved.

"It's Arthur's lizard!" said Bridget.

"You know what I am going to call him?" said Arthur. "Kooky Spooky!"

Huckle and his friends camped in Huckle's house. They slept in their tent all night long. So did Kooky Spooky.

Kooky Spooky was not kooky or spooky, but it sure was a kooky spooky campout!

STERLING CHILDREN'S BOOKS
New York

An Imprint of Sterling Publishing
387 Park Avenue South
New York, NY 10016

STERLING CHILDREN'S BOOKS and the distinctive Sterling Children's Books logo are registered trademarks of Sterling Publishing Co., Inc.

ISBN 978-1-4027-9914-3 (hardcover)
ISBN 978-1-4027-9915-0 (paperback)

Produced by

Distributed in Canada by Sterling Publishing
c/o Canadian Manda Group, 664 Annette Street,
Toronto, Ontario, Canada M6S 2C8w
Distributed in the United Kingdom by GMC Distribution Services
Castle Place, 166 High Street, Lewes, East Sussex, England BN7 1XU
Distributed in Australia by Capricorn Link (Australia) Pty. Ltd.
P.O. Box 704, Windsor, NSW 2756, Australia

For information about custom editions, special sales, premium and corporate purchases, please contact Sterling Special Sales at 800-805-5489 or specialsales@sterlingpublishing.com.

Manufactured in China

Lot #:
2 4 6 8 10 9 7 5 3 1
11/14

www.sterlingpublishing.com/kids

One of the best-selling children's author/illustrators of all time, Richard Scarry has taught generations of children about the world around them—from the alphabet to counting, identifying colors, and even exploring a day at school.

Though Scarry's books are educational, they are beloved for their charming characters, wacky sense of humor, and frenetic energy. Scarry considered himself an entertainer first, and an educator second. He once said, "Everything has an educational value if you look for it. But it's the FUN I want to get across."

A prolific artist, Richard Scarry created more than 300 books, and they have sold over 200 million copies worldwide and have been translated into 30 languages. Richard Scarry died in 1994, but his incredible legacy continues with new books illustrated by his son, Huck Scarry.